Macbeth

Written by Jon Mayhew

Illustrated by Adrian Stone

Collins

Conn

My name's Conn. You won't know me. Nobody does. I'm the lowest of the low in Macbeth's castle. A fetcher and carrier. A runner-after horses. An emptier of bed pans and washer of pots. A boy with muck on his face and straw in his hair. I'm invisible. Nobody sees me. Nobody cares about me. When they tell the story of Macbeth in years to come, they won't mention me. When they sing the song of Macbeth, the killer of kings, the crown-stealer, the murderer of innocents, my name won't crop up in a rhyme.

But I saw everything and I wish I hadn't.

The battle

It started with a battle.

My country is Scotland, and it was ruled by the old King Duncan. My master, Lord Macbeth, was one of Duncan's most loyal, brave and honest lords.

King Sweno of Norway sailed his long boats to Scotland, burnt villages and declared war on our King Duncan. Some Scottish lords joined Sweno but loyal Macbeth led his army against the Norwegians.

I stood on a bleak, windswept hill, holding Macbeth's horse as he ran down the slope with his army. The roar of the soldiers as they swung their swords made me shiver. I looked away when Macbeth's men crashed against the Norwegians like a huge wave against a rocky shore. Metal rang on metal. Men bellowed and arrows buzzed in the air.

The fighting was fierce but finally a cry of victory cut
through the air. The Norwegians ran away across the battlefield
to the distant shore where their ships waited. Macbeth and
his loyal friend Lord Banquo strode back up the hill. Cuts criss-
crossed their arms and faces. Macbeth was suntanned, with dark
hair. Banquo was fairer skinned but it was hard to tell through
the blood and bruises that covered them.

I lowered my gaze as Macbeth took the reins of his horse
from me and climbed into the saddle.

"Send word to King Duncan," Macbeth called to a passing
soldier. "Tell him I will join him soon with great news."

"You want to tell him about the victory yourself?" Banquo said, swinging up on to his own horse.

"Of course," Macbeth grinned. "It will please him to hear of the battle from us first hand."

Macbeth kicked his horse to a trot and set off across the bleak moorland.

"Always hoping to impress the King, eh?" Banquo muttered after him and then followed.

Me? I set off at a jog after them, clutching my lord's rolled-up sleeping blanket and a sack of bread and dried meat. No horse for Conn.

The weird women

It was the middle of the day but the thick clouds made it dark. Rain soaked my rough woollen coat and leggings. The wet grass was slippery underfoot. Macbeth and Banquo rode ahead of me. They looked like two specks of black on a scrubby brown hillside.

I hurried after them but they had stopped and dismounted. I could see Macbeth talking to three hunched old women who squatted around a roaring fire. Banquo hung back.

My scalp prickled. Keeping to the shadows, I crept as close as I dared across the heather and rock. I held my breath and hoped my movements would go unnoticed.

The three old women kept close to the crackling fire.
Their thin, lank hair clung to the yellow skin of their scalps
and the way they grinned made me shudder. The women wove
their long, twisted fingers and swayed together as they grinned
at the two lords.

"Hello, Macbeth," said the first old hag, whose chin was
so long it made her face look as though it was melting.
"Lord of Glamis!"

"Hello, Macbeth," croaked the second woman, warts
sprouting from her long, crooked nose. "Lord of Cawdor!"

Macbeth laughed. "Lord of Cawdor? I'm not the Lord of
Cawdor. Why do you call me that?"

"It will happen, Macbeth!" shrieked the third wrinkled crone.
"Our future king!"

Macbeth looked stunned. "You're mad," he said, in
a quiet voice.

King? I stared at the cackling old women in amazement.
How could Macbeth become our king? I crouched lower,
my heart pounding.

"If you can see into the future," Banquo said, stepping
forward, "what do you see in store for me?"

"Oh, Banquo," sniggered the first old woman, clicking her
fingers. "Poor, handsome Banquo, *you* will never wear
a crown."

The three weird women broke into horrible, croaking laughter and stumbled about, holding each other up.

"Stop!" Macbeth shouted, placing a hand on the hilt of his sword. "How do you know all this? What evil power gives you this knowledge?"

"We are the weird sisters," they laughed. "We see everything!" Their laughter echoed around us, filling my head until I thought it would burst. Then all three women melted into the darkness that had fallen across the hillside.

For a moment, Macbeth and Banquo stood amazed, staring at the dying flames of the fire. I crouched, frozen to the spot.

"They said you will be king," Banquo said, raising his eyebrows.

"And Lord of Cawdor," Macbeth replied, his voice faint. He shook his head and grinned. "I think we had one blow to the head too many in that battle!" Then Macbeth's laughter rang over the moorland.

Even I grinned, despite the memory of those horrible women.

The sound of hoofbeats cut Macbeth and Banquo's laughter short as a party of horsemen galloped into view.

"It's Lord Ross," Macbeth said, raising a hand. "And Lord Angus, too. What brings them here?"

I watched as the lords met, shaking hands and patting each other on the back.

"King Duncan sent us," Ross said, still gripping Macbeth's hand. "He's so pleased with your bravery in battle that he has sent me to tell you that he has made you …
Lord of Cawdor!"

I caught my breath and watched as Macbeth's face went pale. The first of the weird sisters' predictions had come true.

The next king

King Duncan hugged Macbeth and Banquo like long-lost sons.
I melted into the crowd of servants, courtiers and ministers,
waiting to be called for the next job. All the lords who were loyal
to Duncan were there. Lord Ross and Lord Angus had come with
us and I saw Lord Macduff with the King. He was as brave and
trusted as Macbeth.

"Well done, Macbeth," Duncan said, resting his hands on my
lord's shoulders. "Your loyalty will not go unrewarded. Already I
have made you Lord of Cawdor and there is more to come!"

"The old Lord of Cawdor decided to join the Norwegians, thinking they would win," Lord Angus explained. "He has been executed for his betrayal."

"I am honoured," Macbeth said, lowering his gaze.

But I could tell his mind was racing. Mine was too. The weird sisters had said he would become Lord of Cawdor, and it had happened. The women had said he would become king and Duncan had just hinted that more honours would be given to Macbeth. Could it be possible? I could see by his face that Macbeth was thinking the same. Duncan had two sons but he could just as easily choose to make Macbeth the next king. He was loyal, brave and a great general. Why not make him king now?

My heart pounded. If Macbeth became king, then I would have new duties. A king's servant was no ordinary person. Maybe I would live in the palace. Perhaps I'd have a servant of my own! Macbeth was a generous and loyal man.

"My Lords and ministers!" Duncan said, raising his hands. The hall fell silent. "I am old and today has made me realise that a successor to the throne needs to be named …"

I glanced at Macbeth as he listened to Duncan. Was this the moment he became the heir to the throne?

"And so, I declare that, after my death, the next King of Scotland will be …"

Macbeth quivered with excitement. So did I. Hadn't the old women promised him the crown?

"… my eldest son, Malcolm," Duncan said. A cheer went up but Macbeth stormed out of the hall, disappointment carved on his face. I must admit to feeling let down too but I didn't realise how badly Macbeth had taken the announcement.

The next day, I followed Macbeth back to his castle. I was
given a horse as we were in a great hurry. King Duncan had
declared that he would be Macbeth's guest that night and so we
had to make preparations. We galloped across the countryside,
our horses wild-eyed and mouths foaming with the effort.
I thought I was going to fall so I gripped the reins tightly.

Finally we reached the tall towers of Macbeth's castle and I eased my aching body from the saddle. Lady Macbeth stood at the gate. Her ladies-in-waiting surrounded her but she towered over them, tall and strong. She embraced Macbeth and they hurried across the courtyard of the castle and into the great hall, deep in whispered conversation.

I hurried after them but the crush of ladies-in-waiting blocked my path and the door to Macbeth's personal chamber slammed in my face.

Exhausted and aching after the long ride, I followed
the delicious, meaty smell that drifted up from the kitchens.
News of the King's visit travelled fast and chaos ruled
down here. Cook hurried to and fro, yelling orders and swatting
anyone who got in his way. His big red face looked as if it
would explode. The ovens and fires were all roaring and it felt
as hot as a furnace.

"The King is coming tonight and nothing is ready!" Cook
bellowed. "Kill another chicken. No, kill three!"

Servants scampered back and forth, almost tripping over each other to avoid Cook. I crept behind him and slipped a cut of bread from the big wooden table. I even managed to snatch a sliver of meat from the platters that stood near the roaring fire.

"Oi!" Cook yelled and my ear stung from the smack he gave me. "Thief! Make yourself useful and take this drink and cheese up to His Lordship!"

I snatched the plate of food and drink and quickly got out of Cook's way.

It was dark and quiet as I climbed the winding stairs that led
from the kitchens to Macbeth's rooms. As I drew near the door,
I could hear raised voices. I swallowed hard, trying to stop the
tray from rattling. Being invisible was all the more important
when lords and ladies were arguing. I pushed the door open
with one hand, desperately holding the tray steady with
the other.

"He won't live to see the light of morning ..." Lady Macbeth whispered and turned to glance at me. She looked wild, her eyes wide and her mouth tight. I froze and stared at the floor, slowly placing the tray on a table.

"We'll talk about this later," Macbeth muttered and turned his back on me.

Without taking my eyes off the floor, I backed away, half bowing as I went. Then I shut the door and stumbled quickly back to the kitchen. What were they plotting up there? I shook my head. How did I know they were plotting? I didn't know what they were talking about. It could have been anything. It could have been, but deep in my heart, I knew it wasn't.

A waking nightmare

I sat in the kitchen under a table, so that nobody tripped over me. The King had arrived with his guards and lords and ladies following him. He had given Lady Macbeth a huge diamond as a present.

"What I wouldn't give for a jewel like that!" Morag, one of the kitchen girls had said, with a sigh.

"Less of your daydreaming, lass," Cook had snapped. "That sauce is boiling over!"

The kitchen reminded me of a battlefield. Boys and girls rushing around, the fire crackling, Cook bellowing orders. Feathers and flour and pastry and sauce flew all around in the scramble to get each course ready for the banquet. Upstairs, Macbeth was entertaining King Duncan and his two sons, Malcolm and Donalbain, as well as an army of lords and ladies who followed the King around.

"More food!" a pale-faced servant shouted as he hurried down from the feasting hall.

"Conn!" Cook bellowed. "Get out from under that table and take this meat up!"

I scrambled to my feet and grabbed the hot tray of meat. It was best not to upset Cook, and besides, I'd have a chance to watch the feast and see all the lords and ladies.

The servants had a secret passage that led to the feasting hall. It was dark and gloomy with flickering torches stuck to the walls. Normally it was quiet but now people raced up and down, shouting and calling for more food, more drink, more everything.

I was just about to enter the hall when I saw Lord Macbeth standing in one of the storerooms that led off the passage. He looked miserable and angry. Lady Macbeth stood by him, gripping his arm. I pressed myself against the door frame and listened.

"We can't do it," Macbeth said, his voice low. "Duncan is my king. He made me Lord of Cawdor. He trusts us!"

"Then why did you raise my hopes like that?" Lady Macbeth hissed. "You came home full of ambition. Told me I was going to be queen. Now you want to give it all up?"

"I can't do it," Macbeth said, staring at the floor. "What if we're caught?"

"We won't be caught!" Lady Macbeth said, shaking him. "I'll drug the guards. We'll smear Duncan's blood on their faces. They'll get the blame."

"But ..." Macbeth began.

"It'll be easy! Now get back to the feast," Lady Macbeth said. "The King will be wondering where you are!"

I hurried away, dizzy with shock – thoughts buzzing around my head. I wanted to tell someone, warn them. But who'd believe a poor servant boy like me?

Stumbling into the hall, I almost threw the tray on to the table. Cups and plates scattered and drink pooled around the bowls of food. The ladies at the table cried out and a few lords laughed at my clumsiness.

"Watch what you're doing, you oaf!" a servant bellowed and slapped the back of my head, sending me staggering out of the hall.

Tears stung my eyes, partly from the pain of my aching head and partly from realising what Lady Macbeth wanted. They were planning to kill the King.

Macbeth looked so upset and confused. Maybe he wouldn't go through with it.

I hurried out of the castle and into the courtyard. A cold wind blew black clouds across a full moon. I shivered and hurried over to the stables to hide and think.

The stable was dark and the horses snorted, stamping the ground restlessly with their hooves. But it was warmer than outside and I soon found a pile of straw to settle on. Maybe if I told Lord Banquo? He was Macbeth's best friend. But he wouldn't listen to me. And if Macbeth found out that I knew, then he would have me thrown out into the cold night, or worse, executed!

I tried to sleep and forget what I'd heard. Horrible nightmares filled my sleep and I kept waking. The horses kicked and screamed, and the wind howled, battering the roof of the stables.

I woke with a gasp, my heart pounding. I wasn't sure of the time but it was still dark and cold. I dragged myself up and outside. The castle lay asleep apart from a single light burning in Macbeth's private room. I should have stayed away. I should have gone back into the stables and buried myself in the straw until daylight, but I didn't.

I crept up the stairs to Macbeth's room. Every step seemed to echo around the castle, bouncing off the stairs, getting louder with each footfall. I climbed up the passageway to Macbeth's room. The door hung open slightly and the light of a single candle flickered through the crack. I peered in.

Macbeth and Lady Macbeth stood over a table, their hands submerged in a big bowl of water. They rubbed and rubbed.

"See," Lady Macbeth said, scrubbing her hands in the bowl. "It's easy to wash away the evidence."

My head whirled and I thought I was going
to pass out. Lady Macbeth's hands were red with
blood. Macbeth looked miserable and pale.

"We should never have done this," he groaned.
"I'll never rest again. I can see the look in his eyes as
he died even now."

"Pull yourself together," Lady Macbeth snapped,
but she looked white-faced and her hands shook.
"I had to go back and smear the guards with blood.
What were you thinking of, bringing the daggers
back here?"

"I was trying not to think of anything,"
Macbeth said, his voice heavy. "I don't want to think
ever again!"

I swallowed hard. They'd done it! They'd killed
King Duncan.

A loud knocking sound echoed through the castle.
Someone was banging on the huge front gates.

"That'll be Macduff," Lady Macbeth said.
"Get dressed and greet them. They come to wake up
the King and escort him back to his palace."

"I wish they could," Macbeth sighed.

But they couldn't. King Duncan was dead.
Murdered by my own lord and master.

Suspicions

The knocking sounded again. Quickly, I crept back down the passage and out into the courtyard. The first light of dawn was trying to break through the heavy clouds. Lord Macduff's horse stood by the stables along with a number of soldiers and servants. Macduff had gone up to King Duncan's chamber.

"Murder!" Macduff's voice split the silent early morning. "Sound the alarm! The King has been murdered!"

Bells rang and men shouted. I could see servants, lords and ladies peering from their doors and windows, half-dressed, bleary-eyed. Someone screamed. I ran up to King Duncan's room but Macduff's soldiers blocked the way. King Duncan's guards lay at the door, drugged and smeared with blood. The daggers used to kill their king sat in the palms of their hands.

Macbeth strode past me and the guards but stopped at the King's bedroom door. He looked into the King's room and then took a breath. Without warning, he drew his sword and killed the sleeping guards.

"My Lord, no!" I cried out, but my voice was lost.

Macduff ran up and dragged Macbeth away from the King's room. I hurried after, half hoping that Macbeth would confess, half wishing that I had the courage to tell someone.

Macbeth fell to his knees in the courtyard.

"Why did you kill them?" Banquo said, staring at Macbeth
in horror.

"I'm sorry," he said, his voice quiet. "But when I saw
the guards covered in King Duncan's blood I lost my temper!"

"You killed our only possible witnesses,"
Macduff said, glaring at Macbeth.

"Are you mad?"

"I'm only human!" Macbeth shouted.
"How could I stand there and watch them
snoring while their king lies dead?"

But I knew why he'd killed the guards.
If they'd denied being involved in King Duncan's
murder and had sworn that they were drugged, everyone
would have suspected Macbeth.

"You could have waited to see them hang," Macduff said,
coldly, "after a fair trial."

There was a moment's silence. Everyone looked at Macbeth
as if they suspected something. Suddenly, a scream rang out,
making everyone jump. Lady Macbeth had come from her
chamber. Before anyone could say any more, she fainted.
Everyone rushed to help her and Macbeth escaped any more
awkward questions.

It was horrible in the castle. Everyone was crying.
Cook clattered about the kitchens cursing anyone who got
in his way. I wandered around the passageways of the castle.
I couldn't bear to go near Macbeth even if he had called for me
to do something. As I drifted aimlessly, a hand shot out of
a doorway and dragged me into a room.

Banquo stared at me, his blue eyes fierce.

"What did you see?" he hissed at me.

My heart raced and I felt all the blood drain from my face. "Nothing, my Lord," I replied.

"You saw the weird women on the moors, didn't you?" Banquo said, narrowing his eyes.

I nodded. "Y-yes, my Lord," I stammered.

"But you didn't see who killed King Duncan?" Banquo brought his face close to mine. "Macbeth wasn't wandering about in the night, was he?"

"No, my Lord," I said, swallowing hard.

"He's got it all now," Banquo muttered, and I wasn't sure if he was talking to me. "He'll be the next king."

"But what about King Duncan's son, Malcolm?" I said, forgetting my place. Banquo gave me a sharp look.

"Duncan's sons, Malcolm and Donalbain, have fled from here," Banquo said. "They've taken their horses and run. It looks like they had King Duncan murdered."

"Or maybe they thought they'd be murdered next," I muttered, without thinking.

Banquo leapt forward and grabbed me. "Why do you think that?" he hissed. "What do you know?"

"Nothing," I quivered, not looking Banquo in the eye. "I just thought if someone could kill the King, they could kill his sons."

"Be careful what you say," Banquo said, letting me go. "Macbeth will be crowned king just as the weird women predicted."

The crown is not enough

As the days passed by, people began to believe that King Duncan had been killed by his own sons.

Macbeth was named as the next king instead of Malcolm and preparations were made for the great crowning ceremony. Macduff stayed for a few days but he barely spoke to Macbeth. I could see Macduff's suspicious eyes fixed on Macbeth when they ate in the great hall. Not that anybody felt much like eating.

Rumours began to spread, though. I saw people whispering in corners, asking each other questions. Why did Macbeth kill Duncan's guards? Duncan was old, so why would Malcolm have him killed? Couldn't he have waited a couple of years? Some people believed that there was another explanation for Duncan's murder.

The castle wasn't a happy place. Many servants hoped that
Macbeth would send for them to work for him at the royal
palace. I didn't. I wanted to be as far away from Macbeth
as possible.

But of course, I wasn't so lucky.

"Of course you have to go," Cook snorted. Seyton, Macbeth's
chief adviser, had included me in a list of servants wanted at
the palace.

The palace wasn't far from Macbeth's castle, a long day's
walk as I trudged there reluctantly. Cook kept telling me off for
walking too slowly.

"There's to be a huge banquet tomorrow," Cook snapped,
"to celebrate King Macbeth's crowning.
If I'm late for the preparations,
I'll serve *you* up in a pie!"

Macbeth's old castle was a miserable place, but it was better than this dump. The palace was huge and every corner held shadows and whispers. Nobles watched us suspiciously as we came into the courtyard with our cartload of provisions and belongings. Lord Banquo strode past but ignored me.

Macbeth stood on a balcony watching our arrival. He wore a golden crown now, but dark rings circled his eyes as if he hadn't slept for days, and he looked miserable.

"Let's not waste any time," Cook whispered. "Down to the kitchens with you, lad."

Once again, a feast had to be prepared and Cook soon took up his role of yelling and shouting, sweating and mixing.

Seyton put me on gate-keeping duty. Not the big main gate but the side gate that servants came and went through. I had to lock and unlock the door. This was boring work but it meant that I didn't have to go near Macbeth. I watched people come and go. In the afternoon Banquo rode off to hunt before the feast.

Eventually, the deliveries of fresh vegetables and drink stopped and all the servants went upstairs to the great hall or to the kitchen. The side gate and the rooms around it fell quiet. I sat next to the gate, daydreaming, when suddenly, Seyton appeared.

He held out his hand for the keys.

"Now make yourself scarce," he said.

I scurried round the
corner but glanced back in
time to see Seyton letting
out two men. Two men
I recognised.

One was called
Lugg and the other
Ciaran. They were local
outlaws, imprisoned
by Macbeth himself for
highway robbery, possibly
even murder. Why was

Seyton letting them out of the palace? What were they up to?

Once Seyton had returned upstairs, I slipped out of the side
gate and locked it behind me. I could see the men further down
the track that led from the palace. They were heading for
the woods.

Keeping low, I scurried after them. All the while, the blood
pulsed in my head. This was madness! These were violent men
who would cut my throat without a second thought. But I
needed to know what they were up to.

They walked deeper into the forest, meeting a man I
didn't recognise. He looked as wicked and rough as the other
two. They stopped where the woods were thickest.

Trees huddled together here, blocking out the last fading light of day. I crept closer, keeping behind the trunks.

"Macbeth says if we do this job, then he'll pardon us," Lugg said. "He can do that now he's king."

"King or not," the stranger said, spitting, "I don't trust him. I reckon we finish this and then run for it."

"No," said Ciaran. "Macbeth wants to know that this man is dead. He was very particular about that."

The men had chopped a tree down and it blocked the path at this point. They were planning an ambush!

At that moment, I heard horses. Banquo appeared around the corner. I jumped up and shouted a warning but the men leapt out and lunged with their swords. Banquo drew his own weapon and beat them back.

I shouted, throwing stones and sticks and anything else I could find on the forest floor at the villains.

"Get away, boy!" Banquo cried, falling from his horse. "Save yourself!"

Banquo staggered to his feet but the men closed in. In a few seconds, Banquo's body lay on the ground. The men turned, looking for me.

I ran away from them. Brambles scratched my face and tore at my clothes, roots caught my feet and tripped me but I kept running. I didn't stop until I came to the edge of the wood and the palace lay in sight. My lungs burned with the chase and I gasped for breath as I hurried back to the side gate. I was safe.

Wiping the sweat and dirt from my cheeks, I hurried back to the kitchen, only to have a jug thrust into my hand.

"Get that up to the main table now," Cook said. "And don't spill any this time, or else!"

I steadied my breath and carried the jug up to the main hall. Thoughts of what I'd just seen flooded my mind. Banquo was dead, that was certain, and the men said that Macbeth had ordered it. But why?

Maybe because Banquo suspected Macbeth? And Banquo was with him when the weird sisters put the idea of being King into Macbeth's head. He knew too much. Macduff suspected Macbeth too. I wondered if Macduff was the next to be murdered. All these thoughts fled from my mind as I carried the jug into the hall and looked up into the face of Lugg himself!

The ghostly guest

I froze. Lugg stood at the side of the great hall doors, watching the servants scuttle in and out. He stared down at me and I thought I saw a brief glint of recognition in his eye.

Then I was barged aside and bounced back into the corridor outside. Macbeth stood glaring at Lugg.

"There's blood on your face," Macbeth snapped at him.

"Then it's Banquo's blood," Lugg said under his breath, wiping his cheek.

"What do you think you're doing coming into the hall like this?" Macbeth hissed through gritted teeth.

"I thought you wanted to know," Lugg said, with an evil grin. "Banquo's dead."

"That's one thing less to worry about," Macbeth snapped. "Now, get out of my sight. I'll see you get your reward tomorrow. And don't come near the palace again!"

Lugg bowed and swept past, giving me a puzzled frown as he went. I pressed myself against the wall, certain that Macbeth would realise that I had heard the whole conversation.

The Queen came to my rescue then.

"My King," she called, hurrying to him and leading him back to the long feasting table that stretched down the hall. "Your guests are waiting to sit down and start the feast."

I heaved a sigh of relief as Macbeth allowed himself to be guided back to his seat.

"My lords and ladies," he proclaimed, raising his hands. "Please be seated for our celebration feast!"

The guests at the table half crouched waiting to sit once Macbeth had sat down but he stood frowning at his empty chair.

"My King," one of the lords said, pointing to a chair. "Will you not sit first?"

"But that chair is occupied," Macbeth shook his head.

"No, your Majesty," the lord said again, and waved a hand to the chair.

Macbeth stumbled back as if a snake had uncoiled itself
in his seat.

"Get back!" he cried, raising his hands to his face.
"Leave me alone!"

"My King, are you all right?" Lady Macbeth said, grabbing
his arm.

"No," he cried, shaking her off and pointing at the
empty chair. "Can't you see it? Can't you see *him*?"

"There's nobody there, my dear," Lady Macbeth said, in a
soothing voice. "Who can you see?"

"It's Banquo," he whispered to Lady Macbeth, gripping her arm. "Look, he's there! All covered in blood!"

"Banquo?" Lady Macbeth said, looking puzzled.

"You can't say I did it," Macbeth shouted at the chair. "Don't shake your head at me!"

Lady Macbeth turned to everyone in the hall. "My lords and ladies, please be seated. The King has not been well lately. He will recover in a minute."

The guests sat down, slowly. Murmurs ran up and down the table. Macbeth seemed to relax and the Queen clapped her hands. "Some drink to toast the new King!"

I hurried over with my jug and stood by the Queen's seat. Seyton took the jug from me and served the King. All the while, Macbeth sat staring around as if expecting to see some horrible phantom appear.

The Queen placed a cup in his hands and Macbeth stood. "A toast," he began, "to my dear friend Banquo, who…"

Macbeth screamed and hurled the cup across the room.

"Get back!" he cried, turning to his guests. "Can't you see him standing there?"

Everyone stared at the empty spot that Macbeth pointed at. All that lay there was a broken cup and a puddle of drink. But Macbeth glared at the spot as if a ghost stood there.

"My Lord," the Queen began.

"How can the dead rise?" Macbeth yelled. "How can they climb out of their graves and accuse us of murder? Can't you see him there?"

"My King!" the Queen shouted back. "You have guests!"

But I knew what she meant, really. He was giving their secrets away. The lords and ladies stared at each other, whispered and muttered.

"There was a time when if you killed a man, he stayed dead in the ground!" Macbeth said, slipping back into his seat. "Not any more."

"I think we'll enjoy the feast another time," the Queen declared, clapping her hands. "Please leave us. The King will be better in the morning!"

The worried hum of conversation grew as the lords and ladies hurried from the room. Macbeth sat in his chair, sweat glistening on his brow, his chest heaving for breath.

"Banquo's dead, I tell you," Macbeth whispered to himself. "Dead!"

I hurried from the hall, trying to think what it all could mean. Had Macbeth really seen a ghost, there in the room? Or was it his guilty conscience playing tricks on him? Whatever it was, it had shaken Macbeth and everyone in the room. I decided to try and get stable duties, looking after the pigs, anything to get me away from Macbeth.

But the following morning, I was summoned.

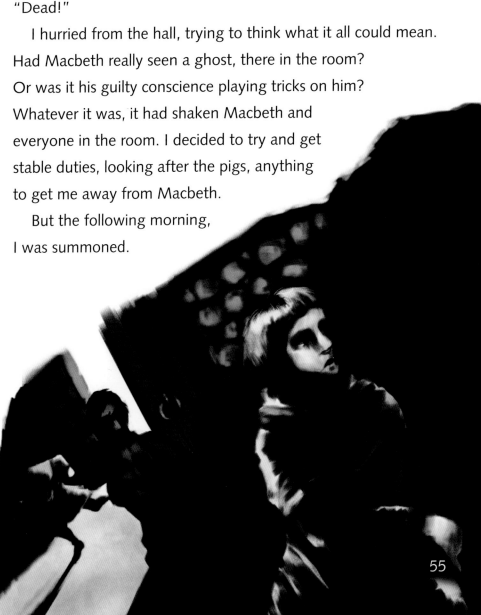

Alone on the moors

Seyton stood by the empty throne and looked down on me. His face had aged, wrinkles furrowed his brow and his hair had gone silver.

"The King is riding out alone," Seyton said, frowning. "He has forbidden anyone to accompany him, but when I insisted that he did not go alone, he said that you might follow him."

"But why me, sir?" I asked, not daring to meet his eye.

"Bad-mannered boy," Seyton snapped. "You go because the King told you to. No other reason. You're nobody. You keep your lips shut tight."

And so there I was, trotting behind Macbeth's horse through the drizzle, across the moors.

For a moment, I almost believed that it was like the old times, Macbeth and Banquo fighting for King Duncan, me hurrying after.

My stomach twisted. There was no Banquo. The man on the horse ahead of me had had him killed.

Clouds thickened and it became dark. The drizzle turned into rain. The landscape became familiar and there in the distance glowed a green fire. Strange figures danced and twisted around the flames.

I watched as Macbeth dismounted and lumbered towards them. Quickly, I hurried after him, crouching behind a rock to listen. The weird women looked as horrible as ever. Their long greasy hair looked green in the flames, as did their warty, wrinkled skin.

"Tell me what will happen," Macbeth demanded. "Show me the future!"

The weird sisters crouched around the fire and threw a strange dust into the flames. A huge armoured helmet appeared in the fire, the green reflected in its glossy metal.

"Macbeth! Beware Lord Macduff!" a deep voice said, and the helmet vanished.

"Tell me something I didn't know," Macbeth muttered. "He has suspected me all along and refused to come to the crowning ceremony."

"There's more," one of the old women said, splashing
a sickly-smelling liquid into the smoke.

"Macbeth will never be defeated until Birnam Wood comes
to Dunsinane Hill."

Macbeth pulled a face. "And what is that meant to mean?
How can a wood move? It can't. So I will never be defeated."

"Not until the trees move!" cackled one of the weird
women. They danced and jumped about, prodding and poking
Macbeth, laughing and shrieking. Macbeth stumbled around
among them and then they vanished into the night. I ran
forward but only Macbeth lay panting on the wet grass.

I stood frozen, uncertain whether to help him up. He stood up and walked over to his horse, ignoring my presence.

My journey back was miserable. All the way home, the weird sisters filled my thoughts. Their evil, toothless grins and dark eyes seemed to peer from every bush. I flinched at every raven's croak, expecting it to be the old women leaping out at me. Macbeth had galloped back to the castle and by the time I caught up with him, I was soaking wet and shivering.

As I entered the palace, a group of soldiers, led by Lugg, passed me at the gate. He sneered down at me and I looked away.

Cook stood in the courtyard shaking his head. "Have you heard the news?" he said, his face glum. "Prince Malcolm is in England, gathering an army. Lord Macduff has gone to join him."

"Where was Lugg going?" I asked, staring over my shoulder at the horsemen disappearing into the mist.

"To Macduff's castle," Cook said, his eyes glistened. "The King has ordered the deaths of Macduff's wife, children, servants … everyone there."

"He doesn't even hide the fact that he's a murderer now," I whispered. It was horrible.

"It won't be long, lad," Cook said, putting a hand on my shoulder. "I hate to say it but Malcolm will come with an army and it'll all be over."

"But what about us?" I gasped.

Cook smiled and winked. "Lords and ladies always need feeding, boy. We'll be safe enough as long as you keep away from the fighting."

Easy for you to say, I thought, but I always get caught up in the fighting!

The figure in the night

The weeks dragged by and I watched the
palace become emptier and emptier. Many of
Macbeth's friends slipped away in the night to
join Prince Malcolm's army, which sat waiting
and gathering men, over the border in England.
Those who were left were too scared of
Macbeth to leave or had nowhere to go,
like me.

Thieves and highwaymen like Lugg roamed
free and terrorised the villages around the
palace but Macbeth did nothing. If anyone
complained, he threw them into his dungeon
or even had them executed.

Everyone knew we were getting ready for
a battle. Macbeth moved us all to another castle
called Dunsinane, further south. It was a grim
place with tall towers and dark passages,
right next to Birnam Wood – the wood that
the sisters had mentioned. Macbeth had told the
sisters that woods can't move, so he couldn't
be defeated by anyone. All the same, I got the
feeling he wanted to keep an eye on Birnam
Wood, just to be sure.

"Back and forth, here and there," Cook grumbled as we tramped across the moors with our cart of pots and pans. "Why can't we just stay in the palace?"

News came that Macduff had sworn to get revenge for his murdered family. Macbeth just gave a cruel laugh.

"How can he defeat me?"

Macbeth looked ill. He'd lost weight and he hardly ever seemed to sleep. Every night I would be sent up to him with drink or food and he would be sitting on his throne.

"I am alone," he said to me once. "I thought being king would be the most wonderful thing but those old hags tricked me."

I stared at my feet in silence and waited until he sent me away.

The passages of the palace were spooky at night. Now so many people had left, they were empty and dead. I tiptoed back towards the kitchens, keeping an eye on the shadows that gathered in corners and around doors.

A white figure stepped out in front of me and I stumbled back. I bit my tongue and tried not to scream.

The Queen stared wildly into my face but her eyes did not see. She was sleepwalking. Her hair looked unkempt and her skin grey. Wrinkles lined her eyes and the corners of her mouth, reminding me of the weird sisters. I shivered.

"Who would have thought it?" she whispered. She scrubbed her hands together just as I'd seen her do that terrible night. "Who would have thought the old man would have so much blood in him?"

I swallowed hard and bit my lip. I pressed myself against the wall of the corridor. She advanced on me, gazing into my face.

"I can't get them clean," she said, holding her hands up. "They're covered in blood."

I slid along the wall, trying to ease past her. She grabbed me by the shoulders. My heart thumped against my ribs.

"Wash your hands, put on your nightgown, don't look so scared. I tell you yet again, Banquo's dead ..."

She let go of me and started to scrub her hands again.

I slipped away and then ran down the passage. I didn't stop until I sat beside the fire in the kitchen.

Rumours of Malcolm's army grew every day. Most of the lords who had been loyal to Duncan had joined Prince Malcolm and he had gathered an army of ten thousand men. I tried to imagine how many people that would be but ended up shaking my head.

"Stay in the kitchens with me, boy," Cook said. "King Macbeth is short of men and if he sees a young lad like you, he may well make you a soldier! The kitchen is the safest place in a battle."

I felt the blood drain from my face. I'd seen battles before and I didn't want to fight in one.

As usual, things didn't go my way. Almost as soon as Cook had said that, Seyton came stumbling into the kitchen with a man who looked like he was about to die.

The man was filthy from riding hard and fast. Cuts and grazes criss-crossed his face and hands. There was no doubt he was one of Macbeth's men who had come back from spying on Malcolm's army. And he wouldn't be back unless Malcolm's army were getting ready to attack.

"You," Seyton said to Cook. "Feed this man. Give him drink. He has brought important news to the King!"

"Yes, my Lord," Cook said, passing the messenger a chunk of bread and ladling some broth from a pan.

"And you, boy," Seyton said, looking me up and down.

My stomach tightened. He's going to tell me to get chainmail and a sword from the armoury, I thought.

"Get up to the top tower," he said. "Tell the King the moment you see anything … unusual."

I scurried out of the kitchen and through the castle towards the tower.

All around me men prepared for battle. I could smell the fires of the blacksmiths. Hammers clanged on iron as they made last-minute repairs to armour. Sword blades scraped on sharpening stones.

Men called out, horses neighed and stamped their feet. I noticed how the soldiers glanced at each other. They licked the sweat from their lips and held weapons with shaking hands. I was glad to enter the dark spiral staircase that led to the highest tower of the castle and leave all the commotion behind.

Sitting at the top of the tower gave me time to think. I scanned the horizon looking for anything unusual, but what was I looking for? A big army, I supposed. But what about the weird sisters' prediction? They said Macbeth wouldn't be defeated until Birnam Wood came to Dunsinane. Well, trees don't uproot themselves and walk, do they?

I gazed out at Birnam Wood that lay spread across the hills in the distance.

No, trees don't move, but these ones did! I watched, my jaw hanging open as branch after branch inched down the hillside.

Birnam Wood was coming to Dunsinane.

The final battle

I hurried down the spiral staircase with
the news of what I'd seen.
I slipped and almost went
tumbling headlong into the
darkness several times.
As I ran, I heard a
woman's scream from
the Queen's chamber.

I tumbled into the
throne room in time
to hear Seyton tell
Macbeth that the
Queen was dead.
She had thrown herself
from the window of her
room to the hard stone
courtyard below.

Macbeth looked old
and tired, as if he realised
that all his plotting had been pointless and he wished he was
just a simple soldier again. I felt a bit sorry for him then but I
couldn't forget the terrible murders he'd committed.

"My Lord," I said, trying to keep my voice steady.

"What news do you have?" Macbeth said, jumping up from his throne. "What did you see?"

"The trees, sir," I stammered. "They're … moving!"

"Liar!" Macbeth yelled, and cuffed me with the back of his hand.

"It's true, my Lord," I cried. "The whole wood is moving towards the castle!"

"It's a trick, my King," Seyton said. "Malcolm's army will have cut the branches down and are carrying them in front of them so that we cannot count how many they are."

"The weird sisters have made a fool of me," Macbeth said, looking into my eyes. "They knew this would happen but they gave me false hope. Well then, at least I'll die with armour on my back and a sword in my hand!"

He strode out into the courtyard where his soldiers stood.

I hurried up to
the tower to watch the battle
on the fields below.

Malcolm's army had thrown down the branches
now and I could see hundreds and hundreds of men
standing in rows. The weak sunlight glimmered on their
armour and swords.

Macbeth opened the gates of the castle and led his army
out to meet the enemy even though they were outnumbered.

The battle was very short. I watched as Malcolm's soldiers
charged, a huge roar rising up to the tower where I stood.
Many of Macbeth's men just dropped their swords and ran.
Others changed sides and turned on their friends.

But a circle of dead bodies surrounded Macbeth. He couldn't run away because Malcolm's soldiers surrounded him. Any soldier who challenged him died.

A strange silence fell over the battlefield. Most of the fighting was over. Only a few men around Macbeth fought on, thinking their master couldn't be defeated. I watched as the crowd parted and a man in bright armour strode through.

"Macduff!" the crowd shouted. "Macduff!"

Macduff confronted Macbeth. I was too high up to hear what he said but Macduff pointed his finger at Macbeth and the fighting began.

It was awful to watch. Macduff fought like a wild animal, slashing and hacking at Macbeth. Then suddenly, it was over. Macduff swung his blade sideways and Macbeth's head spun into the crowd. I watched as my old lord and master's body crumpled to the ground. Macduff had killed Macbeth.

It was over. I felt sad for my old lord and yet glad that the bad times had finished. I hurried down to the kitchen, thinking about what Cook had said before about it being the safest place.

Cook and I sat plucking two plump pheasants in front of the roaring fire. Malcolm had led his army into the castle and declared himself the new King of Scotland.

Macbeth's head was stuck on the wall but I hadn't been outside and certainly didn't want to see that.

"Poor old Macbeth," Cook muttered. "He could have been a great general but he was too ambitious."

"I don't think it was all his fault," I said. "Lady Macbeth pushed him into it, too."

Cook pulled a face. "He could have told her to keep quiet," he said. "He didn't have to kill poor King Duncan."

"True," I said. I didn't mention the weird old women to Cook but I knew they had tricked Macbeth from the start. Everything they said had come true but it hadn't ended well for Macbeth. I felt angry at them but Cook was right, Macbeth had chosen his path. He could've chosen not to kill King Duncan but he was too ambitious.

"Come on," said Cook, picking the last few bits of fluff from the bird. "Better get these cooked. Kings always need feeding, whoever they may be."

The path to power

A soldier

Macbeth was one of Duncan's most loyal lords, brave and honest.

A prophecy

"Our future king!"

A murder

They'd done it! They'd killed King Duncan.

King of Scotland

Macbeth was named as the next king.

The path to destruction

A murder

"Banquo's dead."

A ghost

"Look, he's there!
All covered in blood!"

A prophecy

"Macbeth will never be
defeated until Birnam Wood
comes to Dunsinane Hill."

Death

Macduff killed Macbeth.

Ideas for reading

Written by Clare Dowdall, PhD
Lecturer and Primary Literacy Consultant

Reading objectives:

- draw inferences and justify inferences with evidence
- increase their familiarity with a wide range of books, including fiction from our literary heritage
- identify how language, structure and presentation contribute to meaning
- discuss and evaluate how authors use language, including figurative language, considering the impact on the reader
- provide reasoned justifications for their views

Spoken language objectives:

- participate in discussions, presentations, performances, role play, improvisations and debates
- ask relevant questions to extend their understanding and knowledge
- use spoken language to develop understanding through speculating, hypothesising, imagining and exploring ideas

Curriculum links: Geography

Resources: ICT for creating an advert; paper and pencils

Interest words: lowest-of-the-low, innocents, hag, predictions, loyalty, betrayal, successor, oaf, provisions, outlaws, proclaimed, summoned, unkempt, confronted, ambitious

Build a context for reading

- Read the blurb together. Ask children what they can infer about the setting and the mood of the story from the text and illustrations. Probe them for suggestions about where and when the story is set and about the character of Macbeth.
- Explain that this story is a tale of ambition. Discuss what being 'ambitious' means, drawing examples from children's own experience.

Understand and apply reading strategies

- Read p2 together. Ask children what they can infer and deduce from this prologue, e.g. that Macbeth is a murderer, that his story is famous, that the story is terrible.
- Explain that the prologue is powerful because of the language used by Conn, e.g. 'I'm the lowest of the low'. Check that children understand what this means and ask children what they notice about his narration, e.g. that he addresses the reader directly; that he speaks in short incomplete sentences; that he lists facts to build tension etc.